J Bonnet
Bonnett-Rampersaud, Louise
Going green

$9.99
ocn904604164

To Nicholas and Olga Matthews.
Book and life aficionados!

two lions

Text copyright © 2015 Louise Bonnett-Rampersaud
Illustrations copyright © 2015 Adam McHeffey
All rights reserved.

Published by Two Lions, New York

www.apub.com

Amazon, the Amazon logo, and Two Lions are trademarks of Amazon.com, Inc.,
or its affiliates.

ISBN-13: 9781477847923
ISBN-10: 1477847928

Book design by Lindsey Andrews

Library of Congress Control Number: 2014914201

Printed in the United States of America

THE SECRET KNOCK CLUB #3

GOING GREEN

By Louise Bonnett-Rampersaud
Pictures by Adam McHeffey

two lions

Contents

CHAPTER 1

"EXCUSE ME, EXCUSE ME," I SAID, MOVING Emma's hair out of the way. "Binoculars coming through." I held my binoculars over the back of her bus seat. "I've got to get a good look at those kindergartners. They're soooo adorable!"

I was checking out my possibilities.

In third grade at Lakeview Elementary you get your very own kindergarten buddy.

And here's the thing.

Today was the day!

And here's another thing.

You have to call them buddy even if they throw up all over your brand-new sneakers. Which is what happened to a kid named Adam last year.

Fudgy used his regular eyeballs to look up the aisle.

"I see lots of adorable drool," he said, laughing.

He high-fived The Cape.

"And some adorable boogies," Skipper added.

I rolled my binocular eyes at them.

Those three are the boy part of our club, The Secret Knock Club. The girl part is me, Heather, and Emma. We do stuff like eat snacks and run community-service projects.

And we each have a secret knock to get into the clubhouse.

I took out a piece of paper from my backpack and wrote something down.

"What's this word?" I asked the boys.

"Duh!" Skipper said. "*Kindergarten.*"

"Exactly!" And then I circled the first four letters. "And what does *this* say?"

Skipper looked closer. "*Kind* . . ." he said.

"Double exactly!" I smiled. "And that's what we need to be to them. KIND. After all, the word's right there in the title. We're here to help them learn, people. Their futures are in our hands."

I looked through the binoculars again and spotted a really cute kindergartner with jump-rope hair.

Jump-rope hair is when you have two high-up pigtails that look like jump ropes stuck to the sides of your head.

She was twirling one of the jump ropes around and around like a helicopter. It looked like her head was trying to take off.

I smiled at her cuteness.

"Don't you think you're taking this kindergarten-buddy stuff a little too far, Agnes?" Skipper said. He looked at Fudgy and The Cape. They nodded. "It's not like we're their actual teachers or anything. We're just going to help them read and stuff like that."

Fudgy shoved his last cookie into his mouth. "Well, at least if their future is in *my* hands, it will be a tasty one," he said, licking his fingers.

"Ha. Ha. Very funny," I said. The bus pulled up to school. I watched the fifth-grade patrols help the kindergartners off the bus and walk them into school.

I put my hand on the inside of the window. "I'll be with you soon!" I said under my breath to the kindergartners.

I pulled Heather into the bathroom before the bell rang.

"Can you take those out of your hair?" I asked, pointing to her bobby pins. "I need them."

Heather always has stuff other than just hair on her head. I knew I could count on her. She shrugged. "I guess," she said. "What do you need them for? You never wear your hair up."

"You'll see," I said. I pulled out some paper clips from my backpack and stuck them in my hair. Then I pushed my hair up and held

4

it in place with Heather's bobby pins.

I looked in the mirror. "And for the final touch," I said, grabbing a pencil. "Ta-da!" I spun around. "Teacher hair!"

I looked at Heather.
She looked at me.
And let me tell you something.
Rolling your eyes at a teacher is *not* very polite.

CHAPTER 2

"CLASS," MRS. DUNCAN SAID AFTER WE WERE settled. "I'm sure you all know that today is an exciting day."

I nodded on the inside of my head.

'Cause the outside was full of bobby pins and paper clips.

"After we get through math, we'll go to Ms. Martin's class to meet your kindergarten buddies," she added. She looked up at the clock. "We have about forty-five minutes, so please go to your first station and get started. I'll be calling small groups to the back table in a few minutes."

In math we go to different stations while one group meets with the teacher.

Only here's some news about that.

We don't go to the police station or the fire station.

We just go to regular math stations.

And here's some other news about that.

I didn't even hear her make that announcement at first!

I was busy imagining putting my kindergarten buddy on yellow for talking too much in class.

In kindergarten there's a traffic light system for your behavior. At the beginning of the day, everybody is on green. Then, if they do something kindergarten bad, like talk too much or pick their noses too much, they move to yellow. And then, if they do something *really* kindergarten bad, like hit someone or maybe eat the boogie, they move to red. And then their kindergarten mom or dad has to sign a letter saying: *I've talked to my child about picking his nose too much, and I promise he won't do it again.*

P.S. And I especially promise he won't eat it.

"Agnes?" Mrs. Duncan said. "Are you okay? Everyone else is already at their stations."

"Oh, sorry!" I said. I got up and walked my teacher hair over to learn about all the 'gons. Hexagons . . . octagons.

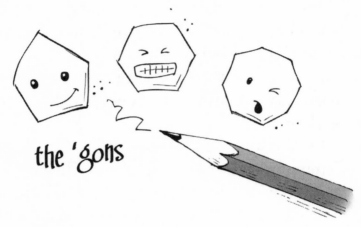

the 'gons

And pretty soon I wished I was gone, too. To meet my kindergarten buddy!

Before long Mrs. Duncan's mouth started moving again, and this time it was saying it was time to line up and go!

She walked over to check the chart. "Let's see," she said. "Who's our line leader today?"

"I am," I said, walking carefully to the front of the line so my hair didn't fall out.

Fudgy and The Cape laughed as I walked by.

I shook my head at Mrs. Duncan. "Kids nowadays!" I said.

She reached for the light switch. "After you, Agnes," she said.

And I walked my teacher hair right down the hall to Ms. Martin's class.

Kindergarten is full of ways to sit.

There's Criss Cross Applesauce.

Or Criss Cross *Pizza* Sauce, as I like to call it. On account of me not liking applesauce.

And there's Magic Five.

And here's the bad news about that one.

You don't get to do real magic, like pull rabbits out of your sleeve or saw people in half or anything.

You just get to sit there.

And not move your arms and legs and mouth.

Ms. Martin's class was in Magic Five when we got there.

They were not moving their arms and legs and mouths for us!

Ms. Martin waved us in.

She is just like Grandma Bling, who lives with our family. Only minus the grandma part.

She wears tons of bracelets.

Her arms look like they're covered in baby hula hoops!

And she wears slide shoes all the time.

Slide shoes are shoes with tippy high heels.

If you look at them from the side, that's what they look like: slides that you could go zooming down!

If you were teeny tiny.

And liked smelly feet.

"Come in, come in!" Ms. Martin said in her excited kindergarten-teacher voice when she saw us.

Kindergarten teachers always use excited voices.

They must learn that in kindergarten-teacher school.

We walked in single file behind Mrs. Duncan.

"Please come and stand over here around the perimeter," Ms. Martin said to our class, pointing to the rug.

Perimeter is a big word for "around the edges so you don't step on the kindergartners."

She took a piece of paper off her desk. "I've already assigned buddy partners," she said. "So, kindergartners, when I call your table, please go and sit down at your table, and I'll have your third-grade buddies come over and meet you. And I have name tags for each of you!"

She nodded to Mrs. Duncan.

Mrs. Duncan nodded back.

First Ms. Martin called the red table.

Heather's buddy was a red one.

Her name was Kate.

She was a fluffy match for Heather.

They both had hair bows that looked like twisty pasta pieces on their heads.

And they were both wearing ruffle shirts.

"You look like twins!" Mrs. Duncan said, smiling. Ms. Martin's arms hula hooped to that news.

Next Ms. Martin called the yellow table.

Fudgy's and Skipper's buddies were yellows.

Fudgy got a boy named Matt.

And Skipper got a boy named Pat.

They had rhyming buddies!

Then came the green table.

The Cape's and Emma's buddies were green ones.

Emma looked at her buddy and smiled.

Her buddy tunnel-smiled back.

'Cause she had no front teeth!

Then it was finally my turn!

My buddy was from the purple table.

I looked at the rug to see who was left.

There were three boys and two girls.

I Agnes-eyed those two girls.

Ms. Martin called a girl named Heather to the table.

And then a girl named Agnes.

An Agnes who was *me*.

I finally had my kindergarten buddy!

And her name was Kindergarten Heather!

CHAPTER 3

KINDERGARTEN HEATHER WAS A LITTLE PACKAGE of perfect.

Dimples.

Freckles.

Chubby doughnut cheeks.

And caterpillar eyebrows.

I smiled at her cuteness.

She smiled back.

"I'm Agnes," I said. "It's nice to meet you." I put my hand out to shake hers.

"Hi, Wagnes," she said.

Wagnes?

I shook my head. "No, it's A . . . G . . . N . . . E . . . S," I said slowly.

"With an *A*."

"Okay, Wagnes," she said, and she opened

her pencil case 'cause just then Ms. Martin started giving an excited-voice direction.

"Third-grade buddies," she said. "If you look at the table, you'll see I've put out paper and pencils, and I'd like you to write your name and then help your kindergartner practice writing his or her name." She started walking around the tables. "But remember, what do we want to use at the beginning of our names?"

The right letter????

"An uppercase letter!" Ms. Martin said. "Our names should always start with an uppercase letter."

Kindergarten Heather said her name out loud. She clapped her hands together twice. "Heath . . . er," she said. "I've got two spillables in my name!" she announced.

"Spillables? Do you mean *syllables*?" I asked.

Then she said my name out loud. "Wag . . . nes." She clapped her hands together again. "Hey, you've got two spillables in your name, too!"

Her chubby cheeks seemed excited by that news.

My slumpy shoulders did not.

Wagnes?

Spillables?

Ms. Martin finished walking around and then went to her desk again. "There is something else I'd like you to do with your buddies," she said, holding up another piece of paper. "This will be a great way to learn a little bit about each other. Third graders," she said, looking at us, "ask your kindergarten buddies these questions. You can write down the answers for them."

Here's what I learned about Kindergarten Heather from the questions:

#1 She is very good at doing her responsibility stuff. She makes her bed every morning and gives her dog, Woofer, a treat before she goes to school.

#2 Her favorite color is red.

#3 She has an older sister who is in the eighth grade. Which is middle school.

Which is when you get a boyfriend. And you kiss him. And that is very gross.

#4 She is never, ever going to middle school.

#5 She has lost three teeth.

#6 She has a BFFN named Melanie. And a WFFN named Claudia.

A BFFN is a Best Friend for *Now* and a WFFN is a Worst Friend for *Now*. (Those weren't part of the questions from Ms. Martin!)

She was just about to tell me about her WFFN, Claudia, when Mrs. Duncan made an announcement.

"Classes," she said, looking at the clock. "We have about five minutes left with our buddies for today." I did a slumpy face. "But don't worry; we'll have plenty of time over the next few weeks to meet again. In fact, we want to make this year's buddy program extra special. Ms. Martin and I would like you to come up with a couple of suggestions for projects you can do together." She turned to Ms. Martin. "And your projects should be related to reading in some way?"

Ms. Martin nodded.

I looked around at Emma and Fudgy and Skipper and Heather and The Cape.

And smiled.

They didn't know why I was smiling.

But *I* did.

'Cause guess what?

A reading project sounded perfect for The Secret Knock Club!

CHAPTER 4

THE SECRET KNOCK CLUB HAD ALREADY DONE some community-service stuff.

First there was the dog show at the Brookside Retirement Village. Then there was the rock-star concert to raise money for the dunk tank at our Spring Un-Fair.

And *now* it was getting even better.

Or at least it was *going* to. Just as soon as I convinced everyone else in the club that we should come up with a plan to make this year's buddy program extra special.

But how?

I thought of Kindergarten Heather.

And her chubby doughnut cheeks.

And I knew how!

'Cause who can say no to kindergarten cuteness?

She could come to our next clubhouse meeting tomorrow afternoon. It would be the perfect time to bring up the buddy program.

After dinner I called Kindergarten Heather's house.

"May I please speak with Kindergarten Heather of 21 Elmwood Avenue?" I said in my best English accent. "I am calling on behalf of The Secret Knock Club and would like to extend a very important social invitation."

I was using my extra-accenty English accent on account of this was club business. I always use my accent for club business calls.

"I'm sorry," her dad said. "I'm having trouble understanding you. Can you please speak up? Do you have a cold or something, dear?"

I spoke again.

"Kindergarten Heather?" he said, still confused.

I nodded. "Yes, you know. Dimples, freckles, chubby doughnut cheeks. About this high," I said, measuring the kitchen counter. "*That* Kindergarten Heather. Is she available?"

"And where you are calling from?"

"I am calling from 325 Wheatfield Way."

He laughed. "I mean, what is this call in reference to?"

"Your child's future!" I said, not very Englishy.

"And *whom* shall I say is calling?" He was trying out his own English accent.

"Third-grade Agnes," I replied.

He paused. "Well, third-grade Agnes, while my wife goes and gets Kindergarten Heather, is there an adult I could talk to?"

"Absolutely!" I said. "There's a Grandma Bling."

I looked around the kitchen.

"Actually, I take that back. She just left. But there's a mom," I said, walking over to the sink. "And here she is."

Mom and Mr. Kindergarten Heather chatted about the meeting tomorrow afternoon and Heather coming to our house.

"You'll drop her off at four o'clock?" I heard Mom say. "That will be great. And of course her stuffed animal can come, too." Mom nodded. "That's right, Grandma *Bling* will be here with the kids. I'll be on night shift at the hospital."

I smiled.

Operation Convince the Club to Make the Buddy Program Extra Special was on!

CHAPTER 5

THAT NIGHT I WENT UPSTAIRS TO BE AN IN-THE-BED thinker and come up with ideas for our project.

I grabbed Rat-A-Tat, my thinking cat, and got under the covers.

Only here's the problem with in-the-bed thinking.

Sometimes you fall asleep.

Without doing any thinking.

And wake up in the morning with taco teeth instead.

"Make it a great day!" Mom called out the next day as I got on the bus.

In our house we don't say *"Have* a great day."

We say "*Make* it a great day."

That way it's up to you how your day goes. And I am almost a professional at making things great!

Well, except for the taco teeth.

When I got to school, Kindergarten Heather and her patrol were in the lobby looking at the fish tank.

I walked right up to them. "I can take her to her classroom," I told Ella, her patrol.

"Are you sure?" Ella asked. "That would be great, 'cause I need to return this book to the Media Center."

"Sure I'm sure," I said. "No problem at all!"

We walked hand in hand down to the kindergarten hall.

Kindergarten Heather stopped and looked through the window of the courtyard on the way. She stared. "That looks like a good place to weed, Wagnes!" she said, pointing. Her cheeks looked excited. Like they were doing a chubby-cheek dance.

"Weed?" I asked, a little confused.

She nodded. "Yeah. Weed . . . a *book*."

"Oh! *Read!* Of course!"

I looked at the courtyard. There was overgrown stuff everywhere. It was worse than my bedroom.

My eyes did a hop, skip, and a jump and then I smacked myself on my forehead.

'Cause, guess what?

Kindergarten Heather was double right! It *was* a perfect place to *weed* . . . and then *read*. It was a perfect place for our kindergarten-buddy project!

I couldn't wait for our meeting later that afternoon.

"A watched pot never boils," Grandma Bling said. I was staring out the window, waiting for Kindergarten Heather.

I checked the clock. It was almost four!

But guess what?

Just then her dad pulled up in the driveway.

"It's boiling, Grandma," I shouted, jumping off the couch. "The pot is boiling!"

I ran to the front door to get my boiling guest.

"You're here!" I said, running to the porch.

"You're here!" I introduced her to Grandma Bling.

"Nice to meet you, Grandma Bwing," she said.

"And who's this little guy?" I asked, pointing to the stuffed animal in her arms.

She squeezed him tighter. "This is Hoppy," she said. "He's a wabbit."

"Well, would Hoppy and you like to go around back to the clubhouse before everyone else gets here? For a personal tour!" I smiled at Mr. Kindergarten Heather. "Thanks for letting her cheeks come over!" I said. "We'll call you when we're done." And Kindergarten Heather, Hoppy, and I ran around the house to the backyard.

"That's your cwubhouse!" she said, looking up at the tree. "It wooks wike fun up there."

I looked up, too. "Yep. That's our cwubhouse. I mean . . . our *club*house."

Kindergarten Heather took my hand. "I wanna go," she said, trotting over to the ladder.

"Wait!" I said. "You'll need this."

She looked down at the pass I'd made for her. I read the words out loud. "Temporary Secret Knock Pass. Good for one admission to The Secret Knock Club."

Kindergarten Heather had confused eyeballs.

"Never mind," I said. "I'll do it for you." And just like that, Kindergarten Heather was in!

Only just then so was everyone else.

They came running across the yard and up into the clubhouse.

The personal tour was canceled!

"We heard you were coming!" Regular Heather and Emma said, jumping up and down. "We're so excited you're here."

"Hey," Fudgy and The Cape said.

"Yo," Skipper said, nodding.

The boys sat down on their beanbags.

Regular Heather and Emma sat next to Kindergarten Heather. And they couldn't stop smiling at her.

And talking to her.

Even after I tried to start the meeting!

"Your favorite color is red?" I heard

Regular Heather say.

"That's such a coincidence. So is *mine*."

I saw her pinch Kindergarten Heather's chubby cheeks.

And then even Emma got in on the action.

"What's your older sister's name?" she asked. "Isn't she in eighth grade?"

I finally cleared my throat. "Excuse me, people!" I said. "We're trying to have a meeting here. You know . . . Secret Knock Club stuff."

I shook my head after that.

'Cause, guess what?

It didn't work!

Regular Heather kept right on going.

"Do you like my bracelet?" she said, pointing to her wrist.

Kindergarten Heather nodded.

In the up-and-down *yes* way.

"I can show you how to make them," Regular Heather said. "We have all the stuff here."

"Stop!" I shouted.

Regular Heather looked up at me.

"Buddy project. Now!" I cried.

CHAPTER 6

I WALKED OVER TO OUR CLUB WALL OF FAME and pointed to the pictures from our dog show and the rock concert.

"Community-service projects are a Secret Knock Club specialty," I said. "We *have* to come up with something good for the buddy project."

Skipper shook his head. "Hold it," he

said. "Mrs. Duncan didn't say anything about a community-service project. She just said to make the buddy program a little extra special. Can't we just give them lemonade or something? That's special."

I had to think fast!

"How are your grades, Skipper?" I asked.

He made a "not-so-good" face.

"That's what I thought," I said. "So maybe if we do something extra special for the kindergartners, Mrs. Duncan might give you extra *credit*."

Skipper thought for a second. "Nah, I'd rather just do extra work sheets. They're easier."

"Really?" I replied. "How many do you think you'd have to do?" I whispered something in his ear. It was his last math test grade.

"Oh yeah," he said. "Good point. I'm in."

"Me, too," The Cape said. "My spelling grade could use some extra help."

Fudgy finally gave up, too. 'Cause we agreed to make cookies.

Three down!

Two to go!

I stared at the two-to-go. "Sure, we're in, too," Regular Heather and Emma finally said.

I clapped my hands. "Great. Now we just have to figure out what to do. I thought we could . . ."

"Weed," Kindergarten Heather said before I could say anything else. She stopped playing with Regular Heather's bracelet.

"Weed?" Regular Heather said.

Kindergarten Heather was announcing my idea!

"She means *read*," I said quickly. "Actually, she means both. We thought we could weed the courtyard at school and make it a place where kids could read. You know . . . a Weed and Read. If you want, we'll make T-shirts with a slogan on it and everything."

"That's a great idea!" Regular Heather said.

I blushed.

"You're so smart for a kindergartner!" she also said.

I unblushed.

She thought this was Kindergarten Heather's idea?

"But it wasn't her . . ." I started to say.

"I wouldn't mind trying to do some posters again," The Cape said. We all looked at him. "You know, to make up for before." He put his hand over his heart. "I promise, no PESTS this time." At our community-service project at the Brookside Retirement Village, The Cape was in charge of our signs, only he'd written "Come see our pests" instead of "Come see our pets." They were "not-so-good" posters.

Even Skipper wanted in.

"I can get some books from the bookstore where my mom works," he said. "She always gets tons of free stuff."

"And maybe we could even compost!" I said off the top of my head. I sang the composting song I'd made up last year when I did the science fair.

It went like this:

"Smoosh it.

Mush it.

'Round and 'round.

Then it goes right in the ground."

Regular Heather said something, too.

And it went like this:

"*What* goes in the ground?" she asked. She looked worried. "What exactly are we smooshing?"

"I don't know," Fudgy said. "But if we get to smoosh stuff, we're in. Right, guys?"

The boy part of the club nodded their heads.

"Yeah, and I guess helping the environment *is* always good," Emma said.

Even Regular Heather agreed with that.

Although she still wanted to know about the compost.

And its smooshy parts.

I looked out the window and pointed. "Come on," I said. "I can show you the real-alive stuff. We're a composting family."

I went down the ladder first.

"Careful climbing down," I called back up to Kindergarten Heather.

"It's okay," she said. "Big Heather's got my hand."

I glared at both of them, then ran over to our compost pile and grabbed some of the dirt. Kind of in a huffy way. Regular Heather was stealing my kindergartner!

"*This* is compost!" I said.

"EWWWW!!! ICKY!" said Kindergarten Heather, scrunching up her nose.

Regular Heather scrunched up her nose, too. "Is that a worm?" she screamed. She started backing up. "I'm sooo out! There is *no* way I'm composting!"

I looked at Emma for help.

"I don't know," she said, looking at the scrunch-nosed Heathers. "Maybe it's not such a great idea after all." She shrugged. "Sorry, Agnes."

And then the boys ditched the idea.

"I guess it does look like a lot of work," Fudgy said. "Maybe Emma's right. Maybe it's not such a great idea."

"*Not* such a great idea? What happened to smooshing things? And helping the environment?" I said. Okay, screamed.

Kindergarten Heather's eyes got big and round at my screaming words.

She grabbed Regular Heather's hand again.

"But hey," Regular Heather said. "At least we can still try her idea." She patted Kindergarten Heather's hand.

I glared at the Heathers.

"Her idea?" I said.

"Yeah, you know...the Weed and Read... or whatever it's called." She smiled.

And here's the thing.

Just then I got mad at two things.

And both of their names were Heather.

CHAPTER 7

GRANDMA BLING CHUCKLED. "*SMOOSH IT. Mush it. 'Round and 'round. Then it goes right in the ground!* I remember that from last year. And I *still* love it!" She looked right at my mad eyeballs. "You're one of a kind, Agnes," she said.

Only just then I didn't feel like being one of a *kind* on account of the double Heather trouble.

But I couldn't.

'Cause it was family yogurt time.

And yogurt people are always calm and kind. Mom, Dad, me, Rat-A-Tat, and Grandma Bling were all yogurting.

"Too bad nobody else loved the idea!" I blurted out. "And too bad girls named Heather can't seem to leave each other alone!" I smacked my forehead. "You should have seen them. It was like they were glued together."

Grandma Bling got down on the ground. "Here, try this pose," she said. "It will help get rid of some of your stress. It's called downward dog."

I covered Rat-A-Tat's ears.

"Do you have to call it that?" I said, referring to the dog part.

Dad chuckled. Then he untwisted his legs.

"What's wrong with downward *cat*?" I looked up at Grandma Bling. "Can't we call it downward cat?"

And just then I had a real-alive downward cat.

'Cause Rat-A-Tat slid off my head!

Yogurt poses are not good for people with animals on their heads!

"The Weed and Read sounds like a wonderful idea," Mom said. "And who knows?

Maybe everybody will come back around to the idea of composting."

"After all, what's important in life?" asked Grandma Bling, looking at me upside down.

"Being flexible," I said.

Grandma Bling always says it's important to be flexible.

But she doesn't mean the yogurt, stretchy kind.

She means the "don't-worry-if-things-don't-work-out-the-way-you-planned, you-can-always-find-another-way" kind of flexible.

"In fact . . ." she said, walking over to the coffee table, "I may have just the thing right here!"

She handed me a brochure.

"This came in the mail the other week. I didn't think it was of any use at the time, but maybe it is! There's only two more weeks left in the program, so you guys better hurry if you want to do it."

And suddenly there was some flexible good news!

TURN 1,050 MILK JUGS INTO A RECYCLED PARK BENCH.

I looked at that brochure and smiled.

'Cause I knew where we could park that bench.

In the courtyard.

That's where!

"Look at this!" I said very proud on the bus the next morning. I held up the brochure. "*This* is the answer to our problems, people."

Fudgy looked at me. "What problems?" he asked. "I didn't know we had any problems."

Is he kidding?

Was he at the meeting yesterday afternoon?

I shook my head.

"Anyway," I said. "What do you guys think? You want to collect jugs and get a bench for the courtyard? It will be perfect for the Weed and Read."

Everyone paused.

"You should probably run it by Heather," Regular Heather finally said.

I looked confused. "But you *are* Heather."

"Not *me*," she said, laughing. "Kindergarten Heather!"

"All right, that's it!" I said in a huffy voice.

"I tried to tell you guys yesterday; she did *not* come up with the Weed and Read idea. *I* did. And *I* came up with the really good composting idea, which everyone liked until chubby cheeks said it was too icky."

I sat back down after my mouth was done being busy.

"Wow, Agnes," Fudgy said. "What was it you said we were supposed to be to the kindergartners?" He nudged Skipper. "Wasn't the word right in their title or something . . . ?"

"*Kind*!" I said, glaring at them. "But that was before . . ."

Fudgy looked out the window. "Well, here's your chance to be kind again." He pointed as we pulled into school. "There she is."

I turned and looked.

Kindergarten Heather was standing outside with Hoppy and her fifth-grade patrol.

I grabbed my "Agnes-does-not-sit-on-bus-seats" towel and tried to hide my face.

Only here's the thing.

Getting off a bus with a towel on your head can be a *little* tricky!

CHAPTER 8

"WAGNES, ARE YOU OKAY?"

I looked up. Hoppy's ears were in my face. And so were Kindergarten Heather's eyeballs.

I grabbed my towel and stood up. "I'm fine," I said, brushing off my pants.

I looked down at Kindergarten Heather's face.

And let me tell you something.

It's very hard to stay mad at cute, chubby cheeks!

And eyeballs that are almost the watering kind.

"Wagnes, are you mad at me?" she asked. Her and Hoppy's heads were both tilted sideways, waiting for an answer.

"Mad at you?" I said in a very mature, third-grade way. "Why would you think that?"

She hugged Hoppy tight. "Yesterday. At the meeting . . . you seemed mad. . . ."

"Oh, that . . ." I said, pretending I didn't remember.

Even though I really did remember.

. . . About the compost.

. . . And the "EWW ICKY" part.

. . . And the "LET'S-RUIN-AGNES'S-PLANS" part.

And suddenly I felt myself getting mad all over again!

But her eyes started getting waterier.

And her cheeks started getting cheekier.

"Oh that . . ." I said again. "It was nothing!"

My mouth surprised me with that news!

And then Kindergarten Heather's mouth surprised *me* with some of its own news.

"Well, I have a wittle surprise for you, 'cause I thought you *were* mad," she said. "I just can't tell you yet."

A surprise?

For me?

I had to find out!

Only just then I couldn't, because Principal Not-Such-A-Joy walked over to us.

She smiled right at me. "Mrs. Duncan told me that she wants to make the kindergarten-buddy program extra special this year." And for once, even her hair seemed excited about something. A piece had escaped from her bun and was blowing in the wind. It looked like it was jumping up and down. "I'm sure The Secret Knock Club has already come up with some fabulous ideas."

"Yes! We want to plan a Weed and Read project, Principal Joy," I said. "You know how messy the courtyard is, right?"

The principal nodded.

"Well, we thought if we cleaned it out, we could use the place to buddy-read." I looked at Kindergarten Heather and smiled. "Right, kindergarten buddy?"

She nodded.

Principal Not-Such-A-Joy reached for the brochure in my hand. "Oh, and is this something you're doing, too?"

She read the flexible news.

Her eyeballs went back and forth over those words like a Ping-Pong ball.

I looked around at the club members. "We might . . ." I said. "We haven't decided yet."

"Oh, you have to!" she said. "You just have to! It would be wonderful to have a new bench out there. And made out of recycled material no less . . ."

And hey!

If your principal tells you you have to do something.

Guess what?

You have to!

CHAPTER 9

MRS. DUNCAN LOVE, LOVE, LOVED OUR IDEA!

She discussed it with Ms. Martin on the way into class, and it was a go. She and the principal were going to get other classes involved, too.

That's why we called for a "let's-plan-this-thing-right-away" Knockturnal meeting that very same night.

A Knockturnal meeting is just like a regular, real-alive Secret Knock Club meeting.

Only at night!

Kindergarten Heather couldn't make this one.

'Cause it was way past her kindergarten bedtime, that's why.

I put out the T-shirts we were going to decorate.

Even the mini ones.

For our kindergarten buddies!

We always keep an extra supply of T-shirts in the clubhouse 'cause you never know when you'll need a slogan for something.

And checked to make sure we had enough paint.

Then I eyeballed the agenda.

"Looks good," I was saying to myself when Skipper showed up.

He held up his jug of milk. "Where do you want it?" he asked.

"In my belly," I said, joking. "We've got a lot to drink if we're going to make it to 1,050 jugs!" I looked around. "But I guess for now, just put it over there on the table."

Skipper walked over and put the jug down.

Then all of a sudden we saw a bunch of flashlights in the yard.

"Ahhh!" Skipper said, laughing. "Watch out! It's the attack of the giant fireflies."

We all laughed.

It was just the rest of the club showing up.

They climbed up the ladder and sat down on their beanbags.

Regular Heather looked around. "Too bad little Heather isn't here this time," she said. She looked over at where we keep our bracelet stuff. "I'd even picked out what colors we were going to use."

"Yeah, too bad," I said.

Although here's the thing.

Those words were not exactly the truth kind.

I looked over at the table.

"Speaking of milk," I said. "Who else brought a jug to drink? We've got to start collecting if we want to order the bench by next Friday."

I looked at the time line I'd written on the agenda. Next Friday was the deadline for ordering the bench if we wanted to get it for grand-opening day. Which was the Friday after that!

"I don't know," Fudgy said. He pointed to the table. "But I brought those." There were lots of cookies all piled up like a stack of books. "After all . . . the best part of milk is the cookies!"

"I'm lactose intolerant," The Cape said, shaking his head. "No milk for me."

"Well, I'm not cookie intolerant," Fudgy said. "Let's get this thing started." And he grabbed a stack of cookies. And poured a cup of milk for himself.

And one for me.

And Emma.

And Regular Heather.

And Skipper.

Pretty soon Fudgy started rubbing his stomach like it was a genie bottle. "I feel sick," he said.

"Me, too," Emma said. "I never want to see a jug of milk again."

"Well, I'm fine," Regular Heather said. "I'm not lactose intolerant yet."

Fudgy's stomach moaned.

And then his mouth did, too.

"That's because you've only been taking small sips!" he said. "Of course you're fine."

Regular Heather smoothed out her regular fluffy dress. "My mom's picking me up early," she said. "I don't want to get sick in the car."

"How much did we get through anyway?" Skipper said from his beanbag. He was hunched up in a milk ball.

I looked over and checked.

"One and a half jugs," I said.

I slumped my shoulders at that news.

Fudgy slumped his stomach. Onto his beanbag. "Oh great!" he said. "Only 1,048 and a half more to go. There's no way we're ever going to do this."

"We have to figure out another way," I said, wiping away my milk mustache. "We can't drink them all!" I rubbed my stomach. "But I think we'll have to do that tomorrow." I looked up at the agenda. "If we can just get these shirts done," I said, holding one up, "we should be done for the night. Just remember to wear them in the morning."

And we all wrote Go Green With the SKC Team on the front. SKC is supershort for Secret Knock Club.

And Weed and Read. It's What You Need! on the back.

"What we *need* is to get home soon," Fudgy said. "I feel like I'm going to be sick. Are we almost done?"

"In a few," I said. I was crossing off T-shirts on the agenda. I looked at the word *flyer* on the next line down. We wanted to make them so other kids would come help clean up the courtyard. "I guess I can handle that later. . . ."

Heather said good-bye and left to meet her mom.

And all of a sudden there was something I couldn't handle right now!

"What are you doing?" I screamed, looking over at Fudgy.

He was pouring the last half of the jug out the window.

Without looking outside.

"Getting us two empty jugs," he said. "Why drink them when we can just dump them?"

"Aren't you forgetting something?" I asked.

"Forgetting what?"

And suddenly there was a scream from the ground.

"That *somebody* had to leave early!"

We looked outside.

At the "somebody-who-had-to-leave-early."

And guess what?

Regular Heather *was* lactose intolerant after all!

CHAPTER 10

"Go Green with the SKC Team!

"Go Green with the SKC Team!

"Go Green with the SKC Team!," we said very singingly as we walked in a row to the front doors of school the next day.

"My kindergarten buddy isn't here today," Regular Heather said. "So I can go and give little Heather her shirt."

She started to pull it out of my hand.

"That's okay," I said, pulling the shirt back. "I've got it."

"No, really," Regular Heather said again. "I can do it. That way you can start passing out the flyers."

"No. I said *I'll* do it. She's *my* buddy."

It was like tug-of-war with that shirt!

"Oh, yeah! Go Green with the SKC Team," Kindergarten Heather said, running over.

"Is that for me?"

And guess whose eyeballs she was looking at when she said those words?

Regular Heather's!

Just then Principal Not-Such-A-Joy came out to see us.

"Let me see your shirts, Agnes," she said. "They look fabulous."

"Why, thank you!" I said, twirling around so she could see both sides. "They *are* fabulous." I kept an eye on Regular Heather when I spun around. "And stay tuned!" I said. "Our fabulousness is about to get even better with these." I held up a flyer.

GRAB A LUNCH AND COME PULL A BUNCH! NEXT FRIDAY DURING YOUR LUNCHTIME.

"We need to hand these out to get volunteers for the weeds. Is that okay with you?"

"A bunch of weeds, of course," I said, tapping the page as the principal read it over. "Not hair or anything."

"It's kind of like a lunch bunch," I said. "Only with weeds. Two Fridays from now." I tapped the page again. "I even used an excited period!" I said. "That's how excited we are about this project."

"An excited period?" Principal Not-Such-A-Joy asked. "I don't think I've ever heard an exclamation point called that."

"I think exclamation marks look like periods that are jumping up and down. Like they're excited! So that's what I call them: excited periods."

I did a little jump of my own, too.

Like an excited Agnes.

"Well, go right ahead," she said, looking pleased. "I've already told the teachers about the project. You can pass them out now to the students."

Only just then Kindergarten Heather started doing something of her own.

Crying!

"What's wrong?" Principal Not-Such-A-Joy said, bending down. "Are you upset about something, honey?"

Kindergarten Heather shook her wet eyeballs.

And pointed to her shirt.

Her very stretched out, tug-of-war shirt.

"Oh dear," Principal Not-Such-A-Joy said. "I wonder how that happened?"

Regular Heather and I stared at each other.

56

Principal Not-Such-A-Joy took Kindergarten Heather inside, telling her that everything would be okay. "I'm sure they'll be able to get you a new shirt," we heard her say. Then she turned to look over her shoulders. "You can start passing out those flyers now," she said. "The bell is going to ring soon."

I handed a bunch of flyers to everybody in the club.

Regular Heather took hers and stood by the flagpole.

Fudgy took his and walked to the bus line.

Emma stayed with me.

And The Cape and Skipper stood by the entrance to the gym.

We had the place covered!

"Weed all about it!" I said, handing mine out.

A few minutes later Principal Not-Such-A-Joy came running back outside.

"I've had some complaints that you're taking kids' lunches," she said. "What's going on out here?"

We looked around at the "out-here."

And saw what was going on.

We all ran over to Fudgy.

And looked at the stockpile of lunch boxes around his feet.

"What are you doing?" I shouted.

He held up a flyer. "It says to grab a lunch . . ." he said. "And I have. A *bunch* of *lunch*."

"Yeah! A bunch of other people's lunch!" I said. "That wasn't what I meant."

Skipper, Fudgy, and The Cape started laughing.

And Principal Not-Such-A-Joy started principaling. "Come with me," she said to Fudgy. "It looks like you and I need to return some lunch boxes!"

Fudgy wasn't laughing anymore.

Things with Operation Kindergarten-Buddy Project were *not* off to a good start.

CHAPTER 11

"WHAT IS SHE *DOING*?" I ASKED EMMA AT LUNCH later on that day.

We were in the cafeteria with the kindergartners on account of it being a half day.

We looked over at Kindergarten Heather.

She was collecting stuff from her friends.

An apple core.

A piece of lettuce that fell out of somebody's sandwich.

An orange peel.

Some carrots.

Parts of a banana.

And here's the thing.

She wasn't putting them in the garbage.

She was putting them in her lunch box!

Emma and I looked at each other. "Gross!" we said out loud.

"My kindergarten buddy told me she was doing that yesterday, too," Regular Heather said.

"Oh, you mean your *other* kindergarten buddy?" I said. I rolled my eyes at that kindergarten stealer!

"Very funny, Agnes." She took a bite of chocolate chip muffin.

"Yeah, my buddy said that, too!" Fudgy said. "And he even saw her pulling up clumps of grass on the playground and putting them in her lunch box." Fudgy shook his head. "What is she doing? Pretending to be a cow or something? I think she's gone kindergarten crazy, if you ask me."

I was just about to go and check on that when the bell rang.

We grabbed our lunch boxes and lined up by the cafeteria doors.

Ms. Martin came and got her class first.

Then Mrs. Duncan showed up to get us.

We were busy talking about my new tattoo when Principal Not-Such-A-Joy walked by us in the hall.

Okay, busy *arguing* about my new tattoo.

I'd drawn it with marker that morning.

"Where did you get it?" Regular Heather whispered.

"At my house."

"I mean, where on your body?" she said, shaking her kindergarten-buddy-stealing head. Her voice did not sound like it believed me.

"Right here." I pointed underneath my hair.

"That doesn't count!" Regular Heather said, not using her whisper voice this time. "You can't get a tattoo in your hair!"

I put huffy eyes on her.

Who was she? *The tattoo police?*

Principal Not-Such-A-Joy stopped us in the hall.

Which was a problem

'Cause she *was* the principal police.

"I'd like to see you girls in my office," she said. She called up the line to Mrs. Duncan. "I'm taking these girls with me for a few minutes." She looked around. "In fact, I need all the members of The Secret Knock Club."

All the members?

Just because I got ink?

And here's something you might not know.

Ink is another real-alive word for *tattoo!*

"Girl with ink coming through," I whispered to Fudgy when we walked into Principal Not-Such-A-Joy's office.

Fudgy did a quiet armpit fart. "Boy with *stink* coming through, too," he whispered.

We all stood around Principal Not-Such-A-Joy's desk.

"I wanted to tell you about a surprise I have for your kindergarten-buddy project," she said, smiling.

A surprise?

We weren't in trouble?

And then I remembered something about that word.

Kindergarten Heather's surprise!

And how I'd never figured out what it was!

I reminded myself to *think, think, think* about what it could be later.

Principal Not-Such-A-Joy continued. "I know you have a lot of the pieces already in place. . . ." She looked at lunch-box-stealing Fudgy. "And aside from some minor glitches, everything seems to be moving ahead very well so far."

We all smiled at that news.

"But what if I told you that I could get an author to come to the grand opening of our courtyard? A brand-new neighbor moved in next door to me last week, and it turns out she's an author. And not just any author! The author of the Zany Andrews Children books. Ms. Mary Appletree!"

We all smiled at that news, too.

'Cause the Zany Andrews Children books are the best, that's why!

"Now, I've already run the idea by her, and I think she's okay with it, even though she says she's a little shy about public speaking. But I thought it would be a nice touch if she received a personal invitation from you guys as well." She held up the phone on her desk and looked at each of us. "So, who wants to make the call?"

There is a word when the principal lets you use her real-alive principal phone.

The word is *jackpot*!

CHAPTER 12

"Sock. Paper. Scissors. Shoot."

We were trying to figure out which one of us was going to make the call.

Sock Paper Scissors is just like Rock Paper Scissors, only no rocks. Just socks! And stinky socks win it all.

We were down to me and Fudgy.

And by the smell of things, he was about to win.

But then he looked across at me. "Just go ahead," he said. "I wouldn't know what to say to her anyway."

"Really?" I said, surprised.

"Really," he said.

I ran around to the other side of the desk and sat down.

"Principal Agnes at your service," I joked,

spinning in the chair.

Principal Not-Such-A-Joy laughed at that part.

Then I leaned back and put my feet up on her desk.

She did not laugh at that part.

I picked up the phone.

The principal dialed the number while I held up one of the Zany Andrews Children books and looked at the picture on the back.

And presto magic!

I knew exactly what to say!

"Hello, Mary Appletree speaking," the real-alive author said when she answered the phone.

"Hello, third-grade Agnes sitting," I replied. "I am calling from Lakeview Elementary." I looked at her picture again. "And I am calling with some good news. I thought you'd be glad to know you don't look a bit like an apple *or* a tree, Ms. Mary Appletree," I said.

There is a rule for getting somebody to do something you want: compliment them first.

"Oh, thank you," she said.

I was off to a good start!

Now it was time to ask her what we wanted.

"We, The Secret Knock Club," I said, looking around at everybody in the office, "would like to invite you to come park yourself on our bench."

"Excuse me, dear?" she said. "I'm not sure I heard you correctly. Did you say park myself . . ."

I finished her sentence for her. "On our bench!" I said. "That's right. Although we don't have it yet. But we *will*. Just as soon as we drink . . ."

Fudgy wrote something down on a piece of paper and held it up.

"1,048 more gallons of milk," I said, reading his note.

I explained our plan to weed the courtyard and get a new bench so we could read to our kindergarten buddies. And how we wanted her to come to our grand opening.

"We'll be celebrating all things reading," I said. "And we figured since you're an author, you might be good at that."

Ms. Mary Appletree paused. "Let me first say I'm very honored to be invited to your wonderful celebration," she said. "But I hope you don't want me to give a speech or anything. I have to admit, I really don't like public speaking very much anymore."

I thought fast. "What about public *sitting*? Do you like public *sitting*? 'Cause we really don't need you to speak. We just need you to sit. And possibly smile for a picture if you're okay with that."

Ms. Appletree thought for a minute.

And it turned out she *was* okay with that.

I smiled at The Secret Knock Club. And at Principal Not-Such-A-Joy.

We had a sitting-and-smiling author coming to our school!

After I hung up I grabbed a piece of paper off Principal Not-Such-A-Joy's desk and put my name at the top. I started writing down a list of everything we still had to do.

From the desk of Princpal AGNES

1. Figure out way to get more jugs.

2. Order bench.

3. Collect gloves and trash bags for weeds.

I continued writing while Principal Not-Such-A-Joy answered a knock at her door.

Ms. Martin poked her head in the office.

"You look a little different today, Principal Joy," she said, smiling.

I looked up and blushed.

"The real-alive one is behind the door," I said, pointing.

"Sorry to interrupt," Ms. Martin continued, talking to Principal Not-Such-A-Joy. "But I have the most awful smell in my room. I've checked all the backpacks and even had the kids check the bottom of their shoes, but I just can't figure out where it's coming from. Do you think building services could spray a little something extra around after school until I can figure out what it is?"

Principal Not-Such-A-Joy nodded. "Absolutely," she said. "Thanks for letting me know." Then she turned to us kids. "It's probably a good time for you to be getting back to class now anyway," she said, holding open the door.

I grabbed my FROM THE DESK OF PRINCIPAL AGNES note to finish up in class.

"Definitely need to talk on the bus later, guys," I said before we walked back into class. "We've got to figure out how to get these jugs by Friday."

Especially now that we had a real-alive author coming to do some public *sitting*.

CHAPTER 13

"Two things!" I said, sitting down next to Emma on the bus. I looked around at the rest of the club. "First, I think we should move the cleanup day to next Thursday. Now that Ms. Appletree is definitely coming, we need to make sure the place is extra sparkly clean. We'll need more time to *spruce* it up." I nudged Emma when I said that joke. "Ha. Get it? *Spruce* it up?"

Nobody laughed.

"But we already handed out the flyers that said the weeding was on Friday at lunch," Emma said. She turned to Fudgy. "Don't you remember? Grab a lunch. . . ."

They all laughed at that.

I pulled out a piece of paper and made a note.

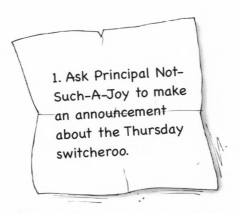

1. Ask Principal Not-Such-A-Joy to make an announcement about the Thursday switcheroo.

"There," I said. "That's done." I tapped the paper. "Now, moving on to the jugs and the bench."

The Cape leaned over the aisle. "Don't you think we should be running this stuff by the Heathers, too?" he asked. "I don't think they can hear from up there."

I looked up the aisle.

At the Heather clump.

The two Heathers were sitting together four rows ahead with Kindergarten Kate. Kindergarten Heather was going home with Kindergarten Kate. They were pulling all the stuff out of Kindergarten Heather's backpack and putting it on the seat. It looked like a garage sale.

"Nah," I said. "They look pretty busy. I'll let them know later."

Suddenly Fudgy stood up. And started counting heads.

Mr. Tim, our bus driver, gave Fudgy rearview mirror eyes.

And let me tell you something. Rearview mirror eyes are WAY worse on a bus than in a car.

'Cause of the huge mirror, that's why!

"Sit down, Fugdy," Mr. Tim said. "You need something back there?"

"Just trying to figure out how many kids are in our school, that's all," Fudgy said, sitting down. He looked over at me. "I have an idea for the jugs."

Mr. Tim shook his rearview mirror head back and forth. "About five hundred, I think."

Fudgy got out his calculator and punched some numbers. "Perfect!" he said. "My plan works."

This was Fudgy's plan: If each kid in school brought in two jugs and then some teachers helped out, too, we'd have enough jugs to get the bench.

It was a perfect plan!

Only then came the "not-so-perfect" part.

"I want to make the posters!" The Cape said.

We all looked at one another.

And then back at The Cape.

"Hey," he said, shrugging. "I promise nothing bad will happen this time," he said, looking around at all of us. "It's only four words. *Bring in your jugs*. What could possibly go wrong?"

Only just then something went real-alive wrong.

Right there on the bus.

"Hoppy!" Kindergarten Heather started crying. "Where's my Hoppy?" She'd emptied everything out from her backpack. And there was no Hoppy.

"Well?" The Cape asked. "You guys okay if I do the posters?"

"I WANT MY HOPPY!!"

Fudgy looked up the aisle. "Sounds like someone's a little un . . . *hoppy*," he said, joking.

73

Regular Heather turned around and stared at me.

"I need some help up here," she mouthed. She waved for me to come up.

"Might be time for somebody to be *kind* to their *kind*ergartner again," Fudgy said, still smiling.

I looked at Kindergarten Heather.

Her chubby cheeks looked like they were melting from all the tears.

I couldn't stand it!

"I'm going in!" I said.

Mr. Tim gave me the thumbs-up to move when we stopped at a red light.

"Wagnes," Kindergarten Heather said, throwing her head across my lap. "I've wost Hoppy."

"Don't worry," I said, petting her head. "I'll help you look tomorrow in school. Hoppy has to be there somewhere." I looked at Regular Heather, who was still holding Kindergarten Heather's hand. "You can let go now," I said, moving her hand away. "I've got this covered."

And we sat like that all the way to the first bus stop.

"I'm just going to go ahead and make the posters," The Cape said, getting off the bus. "And I'll hang them up at the end of school tomorrow."

"Fine, fine," I said, not even looking up.

I was still petting Kindergarten Heather's head.

And then I thought of something. "But wait. I have to leave early for a dentist appointment tomorrow," I said. "So I won't be able to help you put them up. I guess just run them by Mrs. Duncan first."

"No need for that," The Cape said. "I've got it under control. Remember . . ."

"I know. I know. What can go wrong with four little words?"

CHAPTER 14

TURNS OUT THERE'S A LOT THAT CAN GO WRONG
with four little words.

We learned that on Thursday, the day
after The Cape put up the posters.

I was in the lobby with Kindergarten
Heather. We were still on Hoppy patrol.

We'd looked everywhere:

Ms. Martin's class, but it still smelled
awful, so we didn't look too hard.

The library:

Nothing.

Our class:

Nothing.

"Are you *sure* you didn't go anywhere
different the day you lost him?" I asked her.

She shook her head.

"That's so cool," Fudgy said. He was

talking to a kid standing near us. "Can it crawl all the way up your arm?"

Crawl up your arm?

I pretended not to hear those words.

"Just try to think, Heather," I said again.

Skipper ran by us and over to a boy named Matthew.

"That's awesome," Skipper said. "How many legs does it have?"

How many legs?

I also pretended not to hear those words.

But then even The Cape got in on the action.

He walked over to a kid named Jake. "Look at this, guys," he said, taking something from Jake's hands. He held it upside down. "What are you guys bringing in all these for anyway?" The Cape asked. "A science project or something?"

Jake answered. "No, I couldn't find a bug, so I just brought my brother's—"

"MOUSE!" everyone screamed.

The Cape dropped the mouse.

The mouse started to run.

The Cape chased the mouse.

Fudgy chased The Cape.

We all chased Fudgy.

And Principal Not-Such-A-Joy chased us all.

Right into Ms. Martin's room.

Ms. Martin looked up from her computer. "Did somebody say *mouse?*" she asked, alarmed.

"No," I said, standing on top of a table. "Somebody *screamed* 'Mouse'!" I pointed to a plastic bin poking out from behind the book nook. "And there it is! On top of that!"

I pulled Kindergarten Heather up onto the table, too.

And she looked over at the bin.

"Hoppy!" she screamed.

"The mouse is named Hoppy?" Principal Not-Such-A-Joy looked very confused.

Ms. Martin ran over to the bin.

The principal followed.

Ms. Martin bent down and picked up the mouse. "Here, little fellow," she said.

Principal Not-Such-A-Joy picked up a stuffed animal that had fallen behind the bin. "*This* must be Hoppy," she said, walking over to Kindergarten Heather.

She smiled and squeezed Hoppy tight.

"And I think we found the cause of your smell, Ms. Martin," Principal Not-Such-A-Joy said, lifting the lid.

She had bubble-gum eyes!

They were getting bigger . . .

And bigger . . .

And bigger . . .

Like they were about to pop!

"Oops!" Kindergarten Heather whispered. "My suwpwise."

We all walked over and stood around the bin.

And looked inside . . .

At the com-post!

Ms. Martin's mouth came up with a list of words. *Who? What? When? Why?*

"Does anyone have an explanation for this?" Principal-Not-Such-A-Joy asked.

And I must have been the "anyone" she meant, 'cause she looked right at me when she said those words.

Kindergarten Heather hugged Hoppy tighter. Her cheeks turned red. "I made you some compost, Wagnes. For the courtyard . . ."

I smacked my hand on my forehead. "*That's* what you were doing with your lunch box every day!" I said.

Kindergarten Heather's cheeks turned even redder.

And then I thought of something else. "You did that for *me*?" I asked.

And suddenly I felt like an extra bad third-grade buddy for ever being mad at her.

I gave her a hug.

An "I've-got-a-lot-to-make-up-for" hug.

Principal Not-Such-A-Joy poked her head into the bin again.

"Oh, it certainly looks like she did that for you!" She lifted the whole bin. "Let's get this thing outside." She started walking to the door. Then she looked back at the mouse. "But it doesn't explain the bigger problem. Where all these critters are coming from!"

She was almost shouting those words.

"I can explain that!" Jake said, taking his mouse from Ms. Martin. He walked into the hall and came back with a poster.

My eyeballs got big when I saw that poster. 'Cause of four little words.

"What did you *do*?" I said, staring at The Cape.

"What I was supposed to," he said, smiling. "I told everyone to   bring in their jugs."

I pointed to the poster.

"Yeah," I said, shaking my head. "Only this says *bugs*."

BRING IN YOUR *BUGS*!

CHAPTER 15

PRINCIPAL NOT-SUCH-A-JOY USED A WORD THAT afternoon.

It was *pandemonium*.

Only here's some news about that word.

It doesn't mean cute little pandas.

It means crawling, leggy bugs.

Mixed in with screaming elementary kids.

She said we caused a lot of it. The pandemonium, that is.

I was explaining this to Grandma Bling in the kitchen after school.

She'd found the note in a sock on her doorknob.

SOMETHING'S REALLY BUGGING ME.
NEED TO TALK.

Grandma Bling and I have a Sock-It-to-Me program. It's just like e-mail. Only smellier.

She looked at the picture I'd drawn of Principal Not-Such-A-Joy. She was screaming. There were bugs running everywhere.

Also a mouse.

"I think I've seen a picture of Principal Joy like this before," Grandma Bling said. "Only wasn't it ants that time?"

I blushed. "Yes, but that was two community-service projects ago. This time it's bugs. All different kinds. All over the school."

"I see," Grandma Bling said.

"And there's a worser part," I said.

"'Worser'?" She looked confused by that word.

"Yes, way worser." I grabbed one of the nuggets she took out of the oven. "Wait a minute; these aren't toe food nuggets, are they?" I said before I put it in my mouth.

"It's *tofu*, Agnes." Grandma Bling shook her head. "And no, they're not."

I smiled.

And ate one.

"And now back to the worser part," I said, wiping the crumbs off my hands. "Principal Not-Such-A-Joy said we can't do anything with jugs at school now . . . or bugs, of course," I added. I looked her straight in the eyeballs. "So you know what that means?"

"That school will be a little quieter?" Grandma Bling asked.

"It means we won't be able to order the bench in time for the courtyard ceremony! And Mary Appletree won't be able to do her public sitting. And now she probably won't come. And the whole thing is just . . .

RUINED." I reached for another nugget that was not the toe-food kind. "There's no point in even doing it now. Maybe we can just read our buddies a book in their classrooms for our project. Now that the smell's gone, it's not too bad in there."

And then I explained about the whole compost incident in Ms. Martin's room.

And Grandma Bling agreed.

It *did* sound like pandemonium.

"But Agnes," she said, looking right in my eyeballs. "What do I always say is important in life?" she asked.

She wiped away my possible tears.

"I know, I know, being flexible," I said.

"I'm sure if you think about it you'll be able to find another bench to use. It might not be made out of plastic jugs, but it will still be able to work. And the show can still go on, as they say."

Just then the phone rang.

"It's Heather," Grandma Bling said, holding up the phone for me. She put her hand over the part where the words come out.

"Which one?" I asked. "The kindergarten-stealing one or the other one?"

"Just take the phone, Agnes," Grandma Bling said.

It was the kindergarten-stealing one.

I could tell!

But guess what?

She had some surprising flexible good news!

She had an idea how to save the grand-opening ceremony.

With a grand bench her mom had in their backyard!

Her mom said that with a little paint, it would be as good as new.

I "yipeed" at that news.

And also at the *even more* flexible good news.

She said she was sorry for the whole Kindergarten Heather thing.

And here's something *I* said:

That I was sorry, too.

For the whole possibly overreacting thing.

"The show is going on, Grandma Bling!" I said when I hung up.

Regular Heather had saved the day!

CHAPTER 16

THE NEXT WEEK WENT ROLLER COASTER FAST. It was finally Thursday.

Courtyard cleanup day!

I went down our checklist of the stuff we'd collected with Mrs. Duncan.

Gloves.

Check.

Garbage bags.

Check.

Bug spray. ("Or should we call it *jug* spray?" Fudgy had joked.)

Check.

Buckets (the beach kind).

Check.

Shovels (also the beach kind).

Check.

And wibbon (as Kindergarten Heather called it). For the ribbon-cutting ceremony.

Check.

Everything checked out!

It was all in the courtyard waiting for us.

"You're very prepared," Mrs. Duncan said. She was excited by those words. She looked at the clock. "I'd say in about an hour or so Pricipal Joy will call us all down to the courtyard."

"Perfect," I said. "That gives us time for Operation Go Green with the SKC Team."

Our plan was to go real-alive green!

On our faces.

And in our hair.

With green heads and brown shirts and pants, we were going to look like trees!

I'd found some leftover paint at home that could do the trick for our faces.

Plus some leftover spray paint for our hair.

Mrs. Duncan gave us permission to go and get greened up.

"But don't be too long," she said. "We

still have to get that bench painted so it has time to dry before tomorrow. Heather's dad dropped it off earlier this morning."

"We'll be right back," I said. "Promise." And we headed down to the art room. Mrs. Jones, our art teacher, said we could use her room for anything that day.

And this was a very important "anything."

"Come in," she said when she saw us at her door. "I just have to go to the back closet to find something, but you're welcome to start."

I put the cans down on the table next to one that was already there. "Mrs. Jones must have left this one out for us to use, too," I said. "That's nice."

We spray painted our hair.

Then we started going face green.

Only I realized something *after* we were our new color.

There were two "not-so-good" words on the back of Mrs. Jones's can.

Semi and *permanent*.

"Oops!" I said. "I don't think that was for our faces!"

I looked around at my green friends. "Did

anyone use this?" I said, panicked. I held up the can.

No one was *exactly* sure.

Not even me!

"We've got to go!" we shouted to Mrs. Jones, and we flew down the hall. Mrs. Duncan would know what to do.

"WE'VE GONE GREEN!" I announced, walking back into class.

Mrs. Duncan was writing something on the agenda board. Her back was to us. "I know," she said. "I think it's wonderful how conscious you guys are becoming of the environment. And helping to 'spruce' up the courtyard." She laughed. "You know spruce is a type of tree, right?"

She was using my joke!

My spruce tree joke!

But I didn't have time to laugh.

"No!" I shouted. "I mean it. Look at us! WE'RE GREEN!! POSSIBLY SEMI AND PERMANENT GREEN!"

Mrs. Duncan turned around.

And looked at her green students.

"How long is *semi* and *permanent*?" I

asked, jumping up and down like I was trying to shake off the paint.

"Now, now," she said, putting some soap on a wet paper towel. She pinched her lips together. She looked like she was trying not to laugh. "There's only one way to find out."

And she went down the line of her possibly semi- and permanent-green students and wiped a little bit of green off each of our faces.

"WHEW!" I said when she was done. "That was close!"

"Well, good," Mrs. Duncan said, smiling. "Now we can start painting the bench." She opened the back door of the classroom and propped it open. "I have it out here so it will dry faster. Everyone grab a brush, and let's get started." And let me tell you something!

Before long, that bench looked brand-new.

It was going to be perfect for Mary Appletree's public sitting!

Now we just had one more thing to do.

Make the courtyard look brand-new.

Principal Not-Such-A-Joy made an announcement over the loudspeaker.

"Let's go and pick up your kindergarten buddies," Mrs. Duncan said. "And then we'll tackle the courtyard."

CHAPTER 17

"GWEEN WAGNES!" KINDERGARTEN HEATHER shouted when we got to her class. She ran over and gave me a hug. And then she hugged gween Regular Heather.

And guess what?

I was A-OK with that.

Kate, Regular Heather's kindergarten buddy, came over and joined in the hugging, too.

And then we all followed Ms. Martin, Mrs. Duncan, and our classes down to the courtyard. The other third-grade and kindergarten classes were there, too.

"It's like a jungle out here, people," I shouted. "Let's get started!"

"Hold on a minute, Agnes," Mrs. Duncan said. "First, a couple of rules. Remember what they say . . . leaves of three, let it be."

"Let it be what?" Fudgy said, laughing. "Rubbed all over your arms?" He rubbed a regular leaf up and down his arm.

"Very funny," Mrs. Duncan said. "But you won't be laughing if you get poison ivy, Fudgy." She grabbed the bug spray. "Or bitten." And we all lined up to get sprayed.

"Now?" I said, looking up at Mrs. Duncan. "Can we start now?"

She nodded. "Just be sure to take your kindergarten buddies with you to help weed."

I started handing out the supplies.

Gloves.

Garbage bags.

Buckets.

And shovels.

"Everyone, take your buddy and start your gloves," I said like a race car announcer. "We've got lots of work to do."

I grabbed Kindergarten Heather and walked to a corner of the courtyard. "This will be our little spot," I said, smiling.

And we all started pulling weeds.

And things that might have been weeds.

And things that might have definitely *not* been weeds, for what seemed like hours.

And hours.

And hours.

And not just regular hours.

Hot. Stinky. Sweaty hours.

But it was all worth it, 'cause the place started looking so, so sprucey!

And even sprucier when Principal Not-Such-A-Joy showed up with some surprise guests. "I asked a few parents to bring new flowers and plants for your space out here," she said.

And guess what?

Grandma Bling and Mom and Dad were part of the surprise guests!

Dad came over to help Kindergarten Heather and me dig some holes.

"You look lovely in green," Dad said, winking. "Or should I say, lovely in green *paint*?"

I blushed.

Even though you couldn't really tell.

And we spread some more soil and planted more flowers all over the courtyard.

"Oh my!" Principal Not-Such-A-Joy said later, taking a look around. "Isn't this place starting to look beautiful!" She walked over to me. "I wasn't sure you would be able to pull this off. But you've proven me wrong, Agnes! It's really looking fantastic out here! I'll go and announce it's time for the other grades to come down and help. I'm sure you could all use some lunch!" She asked Mrs. Duncan and Ms. Martin to bring our lunches. And then she whispered something in Dad's ear.

"Of course," Dad answered. "Let's bring it down."

And they went to get the bench to put in the center of the courtyard.

"Nobody sit on it today, though," Principal Not-Such-A-Joy announced. "It's not completely dry yet."

And we all sat down on the ground to eat our lunches.

Except for Kindergarten Heather.

Who started running.

Because of a bee.

And I started shouting.

Because of the bench. She was running right toward it!

"Watch out!" I screamed.

But it was too late!

Suddenly our bench was regular green colored.

Plus unregular grape juice colored.

CHAPTER 18

"MARY APPLETREE WILL BE HERE AT TWO O'CLOCK," Mrs. Duncan said the next day.

We were back out in the courtyard putting final touches on the place.

We slapped some regular green paint over the grape juice parts on the bench.

"It should have plenty of time to dry if you go lightly," Mrs. Duncan said.

She picked up some garbage bags that were full of weeds. "And let's get rid of these," she said.

Her teacher eyeballs checked out the rest of the place.

"Everything else looks great!" she said. "And I see you decided to stay in your tree outfits. I think Mary Appletree will get a kick out of that," she said, laughing. "And speaking of Mary Appletree, I think it would be nice if we made a welcome sign for her."

The Cape nodded. "Definitely," he said. "I'm in."

"Yes!" I said quickly. "We're ALL in."

"Great," Mrs. Duncan said. "I have some paper back in the room that we can use. Let's go."

We finished the sign and hung it up outside the front door of the school.

Welcome, Author Mary Appletree.

And guess what?

The Os were apples.

And the Ts were trees.

The rest of the afternoon went speedy quick.

Before we knew it, it was two o'clock.

Mary Appletree time!

Principal Not-Such-A-Joy escorted her down to the courtyard.

We, The Secret Knock Club, stood in a line to welcome her.

We were like a welcome forest!

And I was right! Mary Appletree did not look like an apple. Or a tree. Even though I'd decided looking like a tree wasn't so bad after all.

"Excuse me, excuse me," I said, interrupting. I was trying to save her from doing too much public speaking. "Are you ready for some public sitting?" I asked, pointing to the bench.

Mary Appletree smiled. "That would be delightful, Agnes," she said. "Just like you."

And I blushed.

Even though you still couldn't tell.

Mary Appletree sat down on the bench. "I could imagine reading here every single day," she said, smiling. "Your kindergarten buddies are going to love reading out here with you."

Principal Not-Such-A-Joy walked over and joined her on the bench.

"Hello, neighbor," she said. "And famous author." She gave her a hug. "Thanks again for coming."

Then Principal Not-Such-A-Joy stood up to announce the official grand opening of the courtyard. "This has been the most successful kindergarten-buddy program we've ever had at Lakeview Elementary," she said. "We are going to make very good use of this space." She looked at Mary Appletree. "And to make the day truly wonderful, we have a very special guest with us. The author of the Zany Andrews Children series is here to help us with the ribbon-cutting ceremony." She held out the scissors. "If you would like to come up and cut the ribbon, we would be so honored."

Ribbon?

We started looking through every bag we'd brought. And we couldn't find the ribbon. "No wibbon," Kindergarten Heather said out loud.

Everyone giggled.

"Can we use this?" I said, tugging on regular Heather's head. I took the ribbon out of her hair and smiled at Grandma Bling. 'Cause I was being flexible with my plans, that's why!

"Here," I said, handing the ribbon to Mary Apple-tree. "You can cut this."

Mary Appletree looked at regular Heather. Regular Heather nodded that it was okay. And Mary Appletree cut the ribbon.

And then she did something else.

She said something! In public!

"I know I'm not one for public speaking," she said, smiling at me. "But I just couldn't let this go by unnoticed. When I was a kid, I would have loved to have had a spot at school to read like this. And I heard through the grapevine that there were a few setbacks along the way. But I'm glad to say that through it all, The Secret Knock Club and their kindergarten buddies kept their spirits high and followed through with the job"— she looked around the courtyard—"as we can all see." She held up a set of her books. "In honor of that, I would like to donate this set of signed Zany Andrews Children books to the library here at Lakeview, since you're obviously such dedicated readers at this school." Then she bent down and pulled something out of a bag. "And also this," she said, holding up a tree. A *spruce* tree!

My body laughed on the inside at that!

Principal Not-Such-A-Joy thanked Mary Appletree for her kind gifts.

And here's the thing.

My body laughed on the inside again.

Principal Not-Such-A-Joy and Mary Appletree had both gone a little green, too.

'Cause maybe the paint on the bench hadn't dried all the way, that's why!

ABOUT THE AUTHOR

Louise Bonnett-Rampersaud was born in England and moved to the United States when she was six. She has lived in Florida, Pennsylvania, and Maryland. She received a journalism degree from the University of Maryland. Louise has written a number of children's books, including *Polly Hopper's Pouch*, illustrated by Lina Chesak; *How Do You Sleep?*, illustrated by Kristin Kest; *Bubble & Squeak*, illustrated by Susan Banta; and *Never Ask a Bear*, illustrated by Doris Barrette. The first two books in The Secret Knock Club series, *The Dyno-Mite Dog Show* and *The Spring Un-Fair*, were published in 2012. She currently lives in Maryland with her family.

ABOUT THE ILLUSTRATOR

Adam McHeffey is a musician as well as an author and illustrator. He graduated with a BA from SUNY Purchase College and currently lives in Center Moriches, New York. In addition to illustrating The Secret Knock Club series, Adam is the author/illustrator of two picture books: *Asiago*, which *School Library Journal* called "funny and fresh," and *Rudy and Claude Splash Into Art*, published in fall 2014. Learn more: www.adammcheffey.com.

A SECRET KNOCK GETS YOU INTO THE CLUBHOUSE!

Join Agnes and her friends in The Secret Knock Club as they help with community projects. But watch out—because even the best-laid plans can backfire.

Book #1 The Dyno-Mite Dog Show: Agnes and The Secret Knock Club are doing a community service project at the Brookside Retirement Village. But will the dog show (and canine wedding) be a success? Or a dog-gone disaster?

Book #2 The Spring Un-Fair: The members of The Secret Knock Club learn that the spring fair will be without a dunk tank. So they decide to raise money to rent a tank by putting on a rock concert. But things don't go quite as planned. . . .

LOOK FOR EVEN MORE ADVENTURES OF THE SECRET KNOCK CLUB, COMING SOON!